3·10·10
Cmm-J

Dear Parent:

Congratulations! Your child is taking the first steps on an exciting journey. The destination? Independent reading!

STEP INTO READING® will help your child get there. The program offers five steps to reading success. Each step includes fun stories and colorful art. There are also Step into Reading Sticker Books, Step into Reading Math Readers, Step into Reading Write-In Readers, Step into Reading Phonics Readers, and Step into Reading Phonics First Steps! Boxed Sets—a complete literacy program with something for every child.

Learning to Read, Step by Step!

Ready to Read   Preschool–Kindergarten
• big type and easy words • rhyme and rhythm • picture clues
For children who know the alphabet and are eager to begin reading.

Reading with Help   Preschool–Grade 1
• basic vocabulary • short sentences • simple stories
For children who recognize familiar words and sound out new words with help.

Reading on Your Own   Grades 1–3
• engaging characters • easy-to-follow plots • popular topics
For children who are ready to read on their own.

Reading Paragraphs   Grades 2–3
• challenging vocabulary • short paragraphs • exciting stories
For newly independent readers who read simple sentences with confidence.

Ready for Chapters   Grades 2–4
• chapters • longer paragraphs • full-color art
For children who want to take the plunge into chapter books but still like colorful pictures.

STEP INTO READING® is designed to give every child a successful reading experience. The grade levels are only guides. Children can progress through the steps at their own speed, developing confidence in their reading, no matter what their grade.

Remember, a lifetime love of reading starts with a single step!

For Nora, always our One
—E.W. and M.F.

Text copyright © 2010 by Ellen Weiss and Mel Friedman
Illustrations copyright © 2010 by Marsha Winborn

Published in the United States by Random House Children's Books, a division of Random House, Inc., New York.

Step into Reading, Random House, and the Random House colophon are registered trademarks of Random House, Inc.

Visit us on the Web!
www.stepintoreading.com

Educators and librarians, for a variety of teaching tools, visit us at
www.randomhouse.com/teachers

Library of Congress Cataloging-in-Publication Data
Weiss, Ellen.
Porky and Bess / by Ellen Weiss and Mel Friedman ; illustrated by Marsha Winborn.
    p. cm.
Summary: Despite their differences, Porky the messy pig and Bess the fussy cat are best friends and support each other in all their endeavors, from poetry writing to cake baking.
ISBN 978-0-375-85458-3 (trade) — ISBN 978-0-375-96113-7 (lib. bdg.)
[1. Best friends—Fiction. 2. Friendship—Fiction. 3. Pigs—Fiction. 4. Cats—Fiction. 5. Poetry—Fiction.] I. Friedman, Mel. II. Winborn, Marsha, ill. III. Title.
PZ7.W4472Pq 2010
[E]—dc22 2009013384

Printed in the United States of America

10 9 8 7 6 5 4 3 2 1

Porky and Bess

by Ellen Weiss and Mel Friedman
illustrated by Marsha Winborn

Random House 🏠 New York

1
Perfect

Porky and Bess were best friends, but they could not have been more different.

Porky didn't mind a mess. Bess liked things just so.

Porky lived alone. He liked it that way.

Bess had three kittens. Their names were Two, Three, and Bunky. Porky didn't like children much.

Sometimes Bess would come to visit Porky. "Porky, Porky, Porky," she would say. "Your house is so messy. You should keep it neater."

But Porky liked his house the way it was. He liked bread that was three days old. He liked to keep it on the kitchen chair.

He liked to take his socks off every day and leave them on the floor. Once a week, he picked them up and put them in the wash basket.

Bess didn't like to bring her children over to Porky's house. She thought it was too messy. That was okay with Porky, but he didn't tell Bess that.

Bess's house was perfect. When he
went there, Porky was afraid to touch
anything. The cups and plates were all
lined up, littlest to biggest. There was not
a speck of dust on the floor. All the
kittens' toys were put away neatly.

"Bess," Porky would say, "does
everything have to be so perfect?"

"I like things perfect," Bess said. "The
perfecter, the better."

"I just don't get it," said Porky to
himself.

9

One day, Porky woke up early. He looked out the window. It had snowed a lot during the night. The tree branches were still covered in snow. The big yellow sun made the snow glitter. It made a warm puddle of sunlight on Porky's blanket. But outside, the snow wasn't melting.

It was a good day to stay in bed.

Soon there was a knock on the door. It was Bess and the kittens. "We're going ice-skating," said Bess. "You should come with us."

"But it's so warm in here," said Porky. "Besides, I want to start writing a poem today. The second Tuesday in April is Poem-Reading Day, and I want to have a poem to read."

"Come with us," Bess said. "It will be fun. You can work on the poem later."

"Well, okay," said Porky. But he decided that he wouldn't skate. He would only watch.

Porky put on his boots and his sweater

and another sweater and his coat

and his scarf
and his mittens
and his red hat.

"I'm ready now," he said.

Off they went to the pond. It was very
pretty with the snow falling on it.

Bess and the kittens put on their
skates. They glided out onto the ice.
Really, only Bess glided. The kittens
wobbled.

Porky watched Bess skate. She was
good at it, he had to admit. She whirled
and twirled, she dashed and darted.

"Bess, how did you get so good at skating?" Porky called to her.

"I practice. A lot," said Bess. "I want my skating to be perfect."

"Well," said Porky, "I think it is perfect."

As she did a beautiful backward triple flip, Porky had to admit that even though Bess was very different from him, her way of doing things might not be too terrible.

Sometimes, perfect was not so bad after all.

2
Porky's Poem

Porky was writing his poem.

So far, he liked it a lot. He had written a very nice first line. **I like the warm and yellow sun,** it went.

But what would the next line say?

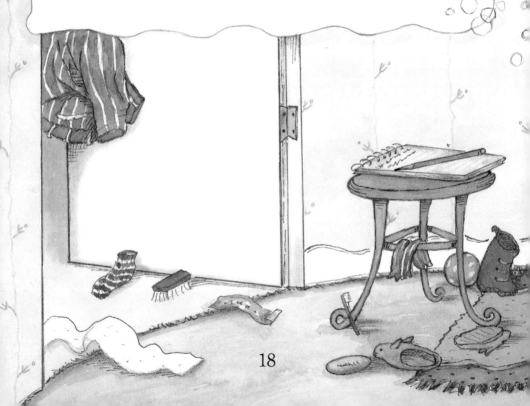

Porky thought about it while he took his morning bath. He was waiting for an idea.

After his bath, Porky sat down to breakfast.

And suddenly he had it!

I like to eat a sticky bun.

Porky wrote that line down before he could forget it.

After breakfast, Bess dropped by.

"Bess!" said Porky. "I'm writing a poem! Do you want to hear it?"

"Of course," said Bess.

"Ahem," said Porky, getting ready. "The Poem So Far."

"I like it," said Bess.

"No, no, that isn't the poem," said Porky. "It's just the part where I tell you that it's the poem so far."

"I see," said Bess. "I'm ready for the poem now."

So Porky read the first two lines.

I like the warm and yellow sun.
I like to eat a sticky bun.

"That is very poetic," said Bess. "What comes next?"

"It's not written yet," said Porky. "I have to wait until it comes to me."

"Let me know when it does," said Bess.

For the rest of the day, Porky waited
for the next line to come.

At last, just before bedtime, Porky had an idea. "Bess is my very best friend," he said. "I'll make this poem be about her." He added two more lines.

I like the warm and yellow sun.
I like to eat a sticky bun.
And when the day is at an end,
I am glad

Porky stopped writing and stared out the window. He was trying to figure out the next line.

I am glad that I know Bess, he wrote. Then he crossed it out. It was nice, but it didn't rhyme.

I am glad that Bess knows me, he wrote next. But that didn't rhyme either. He made a big black line through it.

Porky put on his pajamas and got into bed. He still had a few weeks until Poem-Reading Day. He would think about it tomorrow.

Perhaps the word "end" didn't have a rhyme.

In a few minutes, Porky was sleeping.

3
Porky Keeps Trying

Three days later, Porky sat down again to work on his poem.

And when the day is at an end, he wrote, **I am happy I know Bess.**

He threw his pencil down. "No, no!" he said out loud. "That's no good!"

Soon he might have to give up finding a rhyme for "end." Perhaps he wouldn't have a poem to read on Poem-Reading Day.

4
Moon Cake

On the second of April, Porky decided to make a moon cake.

Porky liked to bake. Baking helped him think, and he thought his best thoughts while he made moon cake. Maybe today he would think of a way to end the poem.

He was going to make the cake just the way his grandmother had done it. He had collected some moonlight in a can, just as he'd seen her do it.

Everything he needed was lined up on the kitchen table. He had flour, milk, eggs, sugar, and sprinkles. And, of course, his can of moonlight.

But when he took the lid off the can, he got a big surprise. The moonlight was gone! Without the moonlight, his cake would not be special.

He was feeling very unhappy when
Bess dropped by.

She knew something was wrong before
he even said a word.

"What happened?" she asked him.

"My moonlight is gone," said Porky
sadly.

"Oh, that is too bad," she said. She sat
down beside him on the sofa. They looked
into the empty can.

Then Bess jumped up. "I have a good idea," she said. "I'll bring you a box of nighttime. I have several different kinds at my house. It won't taste quite the same as moonlight, but it will be just as good."

"What kind of nighttime do you have?" he asked. "Because my moonlight was from a very cold winter night."

"Well," she said, "let me think. I have a box of fancy-dresses-and-orchestra-music nighttime. I have summer-night-with-loud-crickets. I have nighttime-with-snowstorm. And I have foggy-night-on-the-water. I think you can even hear a little foghorn."

"That one sounds wonderful," said Porky.

"Sit tight," said Bess. "I'll go get it."

"I don't want to bother you," said Porky. But really, he didn't mind bothering her to get some nighttime for his cake.

"It's no bother," she said. "My friend Georgina is looking after the kittens today."

Bess went home. In a few minutes, she was back with a blue box.

"Now, Porky," she said, "this is very important. When we open the box, it has to be very dark in the house. Close the blinds."

Porky closed the blinds.

They peeked into the box. Sure enough, it was dark in there.

"Can you hear the foghorn?" asked Bess.

"Almost," said Porky.

Porky mixed up the flour, the milk, the eggs, and the sugar. He set aside the sprinkles to put on top. It was hard to see anything.

Then it was time to add the nighttime. Bess helped him. They were very careful. Then they put the cake in the oven.

They waited.

It started to smell good.

Finally, it was ready. Porky gave Bess the first slice.

"How is it?" he asked her. He was a bit nervous.

"Delicious," said Bess.

Then Porky took a piece.

"What do you think?" Bess asked.

"*Extra*-delicious!" he said. "Different
from moon cake, but maybe even better!"

"I'm glad," said Bess.

It was time for Bess to go and pick up
the kittens from Georgina's house. Porky
gave her some cake to take home for them.

After she left, Porky had another slice.
It was very, very good. He was so happy
Bess had helped him.

What would he ever do without her?

And then he had it. He had the last line
of his poem.

5
The Reading

It was a beautiful spring day, the second
Tuesday in April. Porky's poem was
finished at last. It was time for Poem-
Reading, under the big elm tree.

Bess was there with Two, Three, and
Bunky. All their friends were there.
Everyone was dressed up.

"Ahem," said Porky. " 'What I Like.'
A Poem by Porky."

Everyone clapped. Porky began
reading.

"Ahem," he said again.

I like the warm and yellow sun.
I like to eat a sticky bun.
And when the day is at an end,
I like that Bess is my best friend.

There was a pause while they all thought about the poem. Then they clapped very, very hard. Porky took a bow.

Bess looked embarrassed, but Porky could see that she was happy.